THE INHOLY & UNSANE

AN ANTHOLOGY

John Staunton

Copyright John Staunton 2024
staunton.jb@gmail.com
Cover: Saturn Devouring his Child, Goya

Writing is like being in a cave - I can see daylight through the opening, but I myself am in the darkness.

for Sharon, Matilda
and Woody:
another little book
for you all to
remember me by
when I am no more

POEMS

the hardest part of living	6
the burden of imagination	7
i have found	8
the difficulty of things	9
the inholy & unsane	10
the ugliness of vanity	11
a ghost in life	12
to observe & serve	13
jeckyll & hyde	14
to have known me then	15
i talk to the dead	16
darkness of the night	17
system & structure	18
that fuzzy feeling	19
watch what you say	20
be afraid	21
after we die	22
i do endorse	23
the other me	24
the shopping mall	25

this i know	26
the magic chapel	27
i mourn	28
family is everything	29
watching	30
a purpose & something to do	31
good parenting #1	32
good parenting #2	33
the self-imposed	34
the known	35

<u>STORIES</u>

The Cloud	36
The Senseless Woman	40
The Educated Fool	44
The Panto	47
The Double Act	51
The State of the Art Purposely Built Nursing Home	54
The Rapid Weight Loss Weekend	57

PLAYS & MONOLOGUES

The Undertaker Bros.	63
The Recluse	77
The Happy Death of Reggie Crumb	80
The Burn Victim	85
The Alcoholic	87
The Toilet Cleaner	91
The Dentist	93

the hardest part of living

the hardest part
of living a life | is
the losing & the
leaving behind

the hardest part
of living a life | is
the reaching out &
the staying strong

the hardest part
of living a life | is
the letting go
of the holding on

the hardest part
of living a life | is

the doing | the same
& the same & the
same | & again
& again & again__

the burden of imagination

i think too much

__not in an over
intelligent way |
but in an over
questioning way

i find it difficult
to let things be

as they are | or as
they seem to be

i look for answers
to the questions
that do not
even interest me

i listen to people
talk | and i want

to change all
they have to say

i live in a place
i do not belong | a
place i do not
even want to be

i have found

the people who
pretend to care
are evil people

they are people
to stay well
away from | they

are useless by
nature | and
selfish with self
important plans

they pretend to
know | they
pretend to care

this makes them
unsafe | this
makes them
unbearable
to be around__

the difficulty of things

our
pleasures
in
our
life

are
dependent
on
the
difficulties
of
our
reality

our
difficulties
in
our
life

are
determined
by
the
adversities
of
our
actuality

the inholy & unsane

in the beginning
man created
god | & wrote
a book about it

for the people
to follow &
be controlled

for the people
to accept &
believe is real

for the people
not to question
for the people
to trust is true

a worthless work
of fiction &
unbelievablity
& uselessness

the ugliness of vanity

i see you on
the inside
i see you
looking out

i see you
revealing
what
you want
me to see

i see you
belonging

i see you
hiding
behind the
veil

i see the truth
i see the lie

i see you
believing | &
i see you
waiting __

to be set free

a ghost in life

i am invisible to
the world around
watching people
pass me by__

using my power
of the unseen
silently moving
silently lurking

in the shadows
in the darkness

silently observing
silently learning

remaining on the
outside of things

to observe & serve

i imagined my anus
spoke to me today
the voice was clear
the voice was loud

the same voice i use
everyday | but it
came out of the end
orifice of my mouth

it said to me:

i am your alter ego &
i shall be listened to
for i have authority
& i have a personality

i will have intellectual
precedence
over what you say__

jekyll & hyde

the good &
the bad & the
in between

the unseen
& the hidden
part of me

split into 2

living the
nightmare
instead of
the dream

struggling to
inhabit the
normal | &

let things be

to have known me then

these poems
you see
are already
old & have
moved away
from me

they are from
the other me
the one who
is now not me

to read them
now is
not to know
me now__

they are what
they once
were | & now
they are gone

i talk to the dead

i talk to the dead
of the things in
my life & they
listen to me without

comment | & they
listen to me without
judgment | &

i tell them things

& i listen to their
wisdom & i listen
to their silence &

they wait for me

to join them & they
wait for me with
patience & they

wait for me without
argument | &
with no negotiation

darkness of the night

into the labyrinth
of my mind | into
this tangled mess

i have fallen

the body finding
it hard to hold
the head upright

as i climb

these walls of this
prison | & up out
into the light__

system & structure

ideas & stories
& poems come
easily & come
quickly to me |

it is all the rest
that is hard__

the full stops
the commas
the colons
the semicolons

the apostrophises
the hyphens
the tenses
the spelling | &

the most useless
of them all | the
retarded & the
worthless
exclamation mark

that fuzzy feeling

i am in a fog of a
daze | a grey haze
of a muzzy feeling

thinking all wrong
and unfocussed

thoughts flittering
and unfiltered
with no direction

needing only to
be alone | to rest
and to breath | and

to simply defecate
nothing more
and nothing less__

watch what you say

i listen
i watch
i use__

i take
from
people

they are
my
muse

i enhance
what
they say

i steal

i have
no morals
i have
no regrets

i am a
writer__

i am
not real

be afraid

i want everybody
to know that they
are out to get you

they will take your
freedom & take
your liberty away

they will destroy
you | & they
will silence
your voice | be

vigilant & open
your eyes | stand
up & be strong

we are not slaves
we are not pawns

all this i was told
from a wino__
drinking out of a
brown paper bag
on a park bench

after we die

the soul indeed
does exist | &

after we die
it will leave the
human body

& take a short
journey on
the back of
a unicorn__

before finally
residing in the
butthole

of a leprechaun

i do endorse

i stuck my wet
finger into
a plug socket
this morning

on purpose | not
by accident

and now i feel
wonderful | full
of energy and
full of force

full of vigour
and full
of positivity

like i could take
the whole damn
world on^^^^^^

the other me

__often i am
the other me
the other me
nobody sees

the other me
who is real

the other me
who feels
the other me
who does
not hide | the

other and the
essential part

that is me__

the shopping mall

__looking at all
the shoppers all
shopping for all

the shit they do
not need or even
want | filling up
their baskets and

bags with all the
new things that
will make them
happy | the

living dead fools
that they are__

this i know

i was born
without my
consent

& it makes
no sense | &

the mayhem
& madness
& the mania

is not of
my choosing

the magic chapel

i took my children
into a church once
| only the one time

out of oddity and
out of curiosity

i said to them this
is called a sunday
school where all
the slow people go

and we pretended
to pray and we
kneeled | before

we all left laughing

i mourn

i miss the gone
& the dead
& the creative

they mean a lot
to me | for
they heal me

from the living
& the dull
& the worn__

family is everything

__and when i say
everything | i
mean and include
exasperation and

all other irritations
and annoyances
and indignations

but everything is
becoming more
difficult for me
to disguise and hide

and my frustrations
and my limitations
are starting to show

watching

i saw a woman
on the train
this morning

her eyelashes
were like giant
caterpillars
crawling across
her eyelids

her lips were
like big red
balloons ready
to rupture |

her teeth were
like a newly
painted white
picket fence

it was all very
unnatural |
all very normal

a purpose & something to do

what if all nuns were
allowed to have 1
child (only the 1) &
the babies were given
to the barren people

& all the nuns were
allowed to continue
to lactate & produce
milk | & they were
allowed to pray
while doing this | &

the milk & the cream
& the clotted cheese
& the yogurts & the
ice-cream | was all
sold & all homemade

good parenting #1

i told my son
this morning
over breakfast

that he is half
of me | & the
other half
his mother__

i told him that
any faults or
inadequacies
he has | come

directly also
from his mother

good parenting #2

my son has just come to
me and said: mam
farted in my room and
it smells bad in there
really really bad__

i sat him down quietly
and i said: son you have
now learned a very
valuable lesson in life

think on this before you
ever think of marriage or
cohabitation of any kind

women will do this and
much more before they
are done | for this life is
no bed of roses | now go
back in there and close
the door and suck it up__

the self-imposed

__i sit in exile
and isolation
writing away

a way out
from the world
and from all
around me

not needing
to be read |
but needing
to write__

needing
nothing | only

(to complete
| and repeat)

for the words
to come | and
continue to be

worthwhile

the known

you know who you are

the empty vessels
and the full attitudes

the selective listening
and the moving on

the forever saying
something | and
the having nothing
to say__

the ineffectual and
the apathetic | the
ever so helpful | and

always so far away

THE CLOUD

Willy Blake walked around with a cloud over his head. Not metaphorically. He actually walked around with a cloud over his head. He was not born with a cloud over his head; he was a normal and happy baby - he met all his markers, gobbled up his food and filled his nappies contentedly. At first people could see a small transparent shadow over his head, and then finally, the shadow turned into a full-size cloud.

These days Willy finds it hard to leave the house. He has become a self-imposed loner. He has missed so many appointments and occasions that people often see him as rude by misinterpretation. The truth is: people do not really want to be around him. He depresses them.

"Good morning, cloud," Willy said, as he walked into the bathroom. "Still here I see - which is strange, as I don't feel overly gloomy today." He brushed his teeth and did the usual things people do in the toilet. He then went downstairs for breakfast. It has been a long time since he has had a job. He used to be a school teacher; but the kids drove him crazy with their relentless slagging. "Is it gonna rain today, Willy?" "Where's your brolly, Willy?" "Watch out, Willy, there's a pigeon shitting on your head!"

He prefers to stay home. He is still waiting for some sort of handicap allowance. (They are making it complicated for him - as his condition is unheard of and does not come under usual disability protocol.) He hasn't had an income in over three years. His savings are nearly gone. He has learnt to live frugally. He exists on tins of sardines and crackers. This depresses him more; and makes the cloud even bigger.

He has had many tests to see why the cloud is over his head. He had an MRI scan. The cloud stayed outside the chamber, hovering above it. This seemed a good time to isolate the cloud - but it could not be caught hold of; it dissolved into thin air when anybody tried to touch it. When he got out of the machine the cloud returned to up over his head again.

Willy sometimes thinks that if he'd got married the cloud would not be there, or that it would disappear. But he has never felt the need to be with another person. He's never looked at women in a sexual way; he has never had a sex drive or felt a need to perform sex. When he was a kid he caught his parents having sex, and it repulsed him, made him feel dirty. Actually, it frightened him. He will now only use his penis to pee with and nothing else.

His parents were worried at first about the cloud, but then they got used to it, and learned to ignore it. "Stop moping about all day and do something positive with yourself," they constantly told him. Willy did mope around a lot. He never had any friends. But he wanted it that way. His favourite thing to do, when he was young, was to hide behind the living room curtains and listen to his mother and father argue. He learnt a lot about relationships that way. He learnt he didn't need to be in one.

The first time he was brought to a doctor he was given antidepressants and put on high doses of cod liver oil. The tablets made him feel worse and the cod liver oil made him sick. Today he can't even look a picture of a fish without needing to puke. Then he was taken to see a psychiatrist. She alleged the cloud was a manifestation of his anxiety and guilt.
"The cloud is," she said, "merely your oppressed anger leaving your body and hovering up over your head."
He went every Monday for six months. The cloud only got bigger. He never liked her. She smelled of stale perfume. And more than once he caught her laughing at him.

The cloud remains. The only time it moves any higher or gets any smaller is when he is reading a book. This lifts the cloud temporally. He carries a bag of books with him when he goes out. The cloud stays over his head, but it is smaller. The bigger the book Willy reads - he must actually read it - not merely flick through it - the smaller the cloud becomes. He read *Gone with the Wind* once and the cloud moved far away from him; but when he tried rereading it, nothing happened. He even watched the film - but that had no effect on the cloud whatsoever.

Yesterday Willy tried to kill himself. I'm a complete failure, he thought, I can't even do one simple thing right. He took a load of sleeping tablets and a bottle of cough medicine. The cough mixture made him sick and the tablets ended up in the toilet bowl. He didn't want to die; he just wanted the cloud to go away, to disappear. He is tired of people staring and pointing at him every time he leaves the house.

He read a magazine article called *Weather: And the Affect it has on People.* It said SAD (Seasonal Affective Disorder) was very real. People who suffer from it can have low energy, problems sleeping, and lose pleasure in things - at certain times of the year - mainly in winter. Less daylight, it stated, sets off a chemical change in the brain leading to depression. It said Light Therapy was a way to eradicate the disorder.

The article gave Willy hope. It was very educational. He went out and bought a load of vitamin D and melatonin tablets; and he purchased a second-hand high-level UV sun-bed. He spent many hours a day on the sun-bed (the cloud remained outside floating above it). After a few weeks he developed burns all over his body; he looked like a boiled lobster. The tablets did not work either; the cloud stayed over his head.
And thoughts of suicide prevailed yet again.

Then, one day he was out walking in the street - with his head low and the cloud up above him - when a tall, handsome man approached him.
"Excuse me," the man said, "I can't help notice that you've got a cloud over your head; would you let me examine you?"
Willy was confused, he wondered why an attractive, well-dressed man, would want to examine him. He blushed, turning bright red (which was very noticeable on top of the sunburn.)
"Do you not recognize me from TV," the man said, "I'm Doug Harper; I do the weather report, after the news, for Chanel 6" He had a wonderful head of golden hair. His voice was strong, full of gravitas and experience.
"I can help you, if you allow me," he reassured Willy.

To cut a long story short: Willy is no longer depressed. In fact, he's happier than he's ever been in his whole life. Doug and Willy is now a happily married couple. Willy mopes around a lot less these days; he's more gregarious, bubblier. Doug has introduced him to the new wonders of delicious food; and to the pleasures of the flesh.

The cloud has now gone.

At first there was persistent rain over their double bed - and then one night - the cloud simply disappeared into thin air. Or as Doug would say: "The floating mass of H_2O particles have dissipated due to greater evaporation than condensation."

You see, Doug Harper is much more than just a good-looking weatherman: He is a sexy meteorologist. And - in this new and hot and steamy environment - the cloud remains no more.

THE SENSELESS WOMAN

I bought myself a pair of rose tinted glasses last week. And today I got myself a pair of earplugs. I don't want to see things as they really are anymore. The peace and quiet at the moment is heavenly. No intrusion from the outside world. I see no dust around the house; and I can't hear all the kids screaming out on the street. Bliss.

That's two senses less. And I'm a lot happier. I don't have to look at my husband's ugly face in the full light of day. I don't have to listen to him moan all day long. He's retarded, I mean, retired. It's terrible. The two of us in the house all day getting on each other's nerves, breathing the same air as each other. We have been married almost forty-five years. That's a horrible, depressing thought. The rose tinted glasses and the ear plugs may just prevent me from murdering the bastard.

I could see Sid's lips move. He was trying to ask me something. I removed one of the earplugs.
'I'm going out for a few hours,' he said, 'do you need anything?'
'That's all I need, thanks,' I replied.
To get shut of him is wonderful. He just creeps around the house all day playing that nasty music of his. Bob Dylan and Leonard bloody Cohen. Whoever told those men they could sing! It's excruciating with the earplugs not in.
I'm going to do some well-needed hovering now; and then sit down and have a nice cup of tea and some raspberry pavlova, and listen to that sexy voice of Pavarotti.

Every Friday he goes out to collect his pension. He'll come home at six O' clock with his newspaper and a pouch of tobacco. He's a pipe man (he thinks he looks like Sherlock Holmes). I don't know where he goes or what he does when he goes out - I'm just glad to get rid of him for the few hours. He'll never bring home a loaf of bread or a carton of milk. He thinks that stuff appears in the house by magic.

I should be a little nicer to Sid as he's waiting to be called into hospital for a heart operation. I think a double bypass. (I'm not fully sure as I couldn't really hear him tell me all the details with my earplugs in). They said he'll need a lot of aftercare when he comes home. If he comes home. I'll be tempted to put a pillow over his face if it all gets too much.

'I'm very worried about this operation you've got to have,' Becky told Sid, as she lay in bed beside him in the hotel room. 'Will we still be able to see each other every Friday? What if your wife wants to keep you at home all the time?'

'Don't worry, my darling,' said Sid, 'nothing can separate us. You are my whole world. I live for these Friday afternoons we spend together.'

'I'm so much younger than you. I look up to you. I want you to keep teaching me new things. You've opened my mind up to such amazing things like old B&W movies and actual books. I worry that someday you might get bored with me?'

'Never,' my angel,' said Sid. 'I'm the luckiest man alive to have found you. And you have introduced me to loads of wonderful things like TikTok and bubble-gum flavour vapes. You've added twenty years to my life. After the operation - I will be a new man - and we can be together every day.'

'You really mean it?'

'I've never loved Angela the way I love you. The huge age gap between you and me means absolutely nothing.

'Is she still not sleeping with you?'

'She never had any interest in that side of the relationship. Sex was a chore for her, something to get over and done with. The only time she ever had an orgasm was when I bought her a new hover for her birthday. She was ecstatic. It used to be headaches, now she won't even let me touch her. She says when I touch her it makes her skin crawl. And she's lost all interest in her appearance, she just sits around all day in that old tattered dressing gown.'

Becky pulled Sid closer as she fondled his nipples.

'Well, we've no problem in that department,' she said, as she cuddled up naked beside him, 'as far as I'm concerned you're a proper little horny bunny rabbit for your age!' They then made love for a second time before it was time to check out.

The next night Angela went to the opera to see Madame Butterfly. She loved to sit by herself and sing along at the opera.

Sid was at home reading a book when he got severe chest pains. He made it to the phone to ring an ambulance. When Angela got home a neighbour told her what had happened and where he was. She was tired after the opera and she took a glass of red wine up to bed with her. She would ring the hospital in the morning.

'I'm calling to see how my husband is, his name is Sid Clooney, I'm his wife Angela; he was taken in yesterday evening.'

'Yes. He's in ICU at the moment, a nurse said, the operation is all over; he is sleeping and we're managing his pain.'

'Was it a double bypass?'

'He had a quadruple bypass; but he's over the worst and out of danger at the moment'

'Should I drop in to see him,' asked Angela.

'Maybe later today; he is doing fine; his daughter is in with him; she sat holding his hand all through the night.'

Angela hung up the phone. 'The nurse is confused,' she thought, 'we haven't got a daughter; we've no children at all!'

Becky lay on the hospital bed beside Sid.

She was so young and so full of life. She had beautiful long blond hair and blindingly white teeth. She was beautiful, but a little insecure. She mistakenly believed her breasts were too big. Sid had to constantly reassure her that they were absolutely not.

Sid woke up slowly. He looked awful with all the tubes hanging out of him, all the machines around him.

'As soon as I'm out of here, darling, we'll move in together, he told Becky. 'Angela and I are finished. I think she may be going deaf,' he continued, 'she hears nothing I say to her lately. And she has on these pink glasses all the time; she looks ridiculous.'

'She's no good for you, Sid; it's our time now. She never really loved you; you have me now.'

Becky removed Sid's oxygen mask and passionately kissed him on the lips. As he slipped in and out of consciousness they made plans for their future together.

'Yes, my darling, forget Friday afternoons,' Sid mumbled to her, 'soon, every day will be our day.'

Two years later. Sid's heart is stronger than ever. Becky looks after his every need, his every desire. They are happy together. Sid has lost a lot of weight and he looks terrific. In a couple of weeks, he's going to Turkey to get new hair plugs put in.

Angel's funeral was six months ago. She had developed severe hearing loss and blurred vision. The doctors finally discovered she had a brain tumour; when it was taken out it was the size of a small grapefruit or orange. After the surgery she suffered from amnesia (she no longer recognized her husband), and she lost her sense of smell and taste. One day she had a seizure and broke one of her hips; nobody knew it was broken until she tried to stand up the following day. In the end things were extremely isolating for her: the hearing loss, the near blindness, the no smell or taste - and not letting anybody touch her.

It was a small funeral. No fuss. A short service followed by a quick burning. Sid laid her to rest in her dressing gown and her pink glasses. Hallelujah, by Leonard Cohen, was played as the curtains closed in front of the coffin.

THE EDUCATED FOOL

"See you - you rotten bastard - I hope you burn in bloody hell," she roared at me through the office door before slamming it shut and fucking off. Her name is Helen; but I call her CUNT. Everybody hates her, but she hasn't a clue about that. Actually, she hasn't a clue about anything. She's as dumb as a bag of bricks. And as ugly as a bucket of rotten fish heads.

She's my receptionist in my chiropodist clinic. It's not a real job; it's a community employment scheme. I took her on by mistake. Once she got her foot in the door I couldn't get rid of her. She's a horrible person. Her whole family is rotten. They've all done jail time. I have lost most of my customers over of her. If I ask her to do anything, she'll look at me angrily and say "I'll get my son after you!" I've seen photos of him: a body covered in tattoos and a face like a constipated pit-bull. The whole family look like they're inbred and uneducated. A deadly mix.

Most of the time I have to answer the phone myself. Every twenty minutes or so she takes a cigarette break. I fantasise about her getting cancer and dying - but that could take years. I'm trapped. I shouldn't have given her the job; I did so because I got her for nothing - but now my business is in ruin. She takes money from the till and robs the toilet rolls.

For such a little woman (4 foot nothing) she has a big mouth; as filthy as an overflowing sewer. A real example of the runt of the litter. A fighting little mongrel bitch. I truly believe she has the evil gene: an evil gene that's been handed down through the generations. It's not survival of the fittest in this world; it's survival of the roughest.
"You're not street-smart like me," she tells me, in that piercing voice of hers, "you're just an educated fool!"

She could teach classes in laziness, but that would be too much work for her. A born loafer. She watches videos on TikTok all day. And she never stops eating. Put any food in front of her and she'll lap it up; actually, put it behind her or to the right or to the left of her, and she'll lap it up. "I've a huge metabolism," she says, "I can eat all kinds of shit and it has no effect on me." She's short and stocky; she looks like a beach ball with clothes on.

"I don't know why I'm even here," she tells me, "there's no work for me; I could easily stay in bed and take the crap wage without havin' to come in here every day!" A lot of the time she does stay in bed. She could be in the Guinness Book of Records for the most days missed in a year. Not sick, just debilitating laziness. She'd be proud of that. "Did you see me in that big book - I'm a celebrity, I am."

I'm at my wits end. Her vulgarity is obvious to everyone. I have even turned crude by association. To be honest, I'm scared of her. When she gets mad and shouts obscenities at me, her false teeth move in her mouth, and she ends up spitting at me. And her hacking cough frightens the customers. The constant stream of phlegm and fluids that emanate from her is degusting.

I always wanted to be a chiropodist. (I started out as a proctologist; but I very quickly got bored looking up people's bumholes.) I've always been attracted to feet, and was happy to become a podiatrist. I love feet - *sexy* feet - not the type I see in here every day. Nails as tough as elk antlers and rhino tusks (I have to use an 18-inch hacksaw to cut through them); cracked heels with barnacles clinging to them; toes with cauliflowers and cabbages growing in between them. The odd time I'll get presented with the triple whammy of foot problems: Bacteria, Fungus and Yeast infection. It's safe to say, I no longer have a foot fetish.

"When are you gonna look at *my* feet?" my horrible receptionist keeps asking me, "They're fuckin' killing me!" I often think of poisoning her with the acid I use for the corns and the warts. I need to get rid of her; but I am not going to do jail time over her. I will think of something. I will not be defeated.

Today I decided to have a look at her feet. Bunions. She had been squashing her size 7 feet into size 3 shoes her whole life.

I had a light bulb moment. This was my chance.

"I can break your feet for you," I told her, "and I can re-set them again for you."

"What'll it cost," she said, "and will it hurt?"

"It'll cost you nothing; I will foot the bill," I told her. And you won't feel a thing," I reassured her, "I have plenty of stuff here to knock you out with."

So I broke both her feet and I re-set them.

I made her sign a weaver beforehand in case anything should go wrong. She woke up screaming in the middle of the procedure - but I gave her more gas and got her back to sleep. She will need to have proper surgery to have pins and plates inserted; her feet are now no longer able to support her weight. The damage is irreparable. She'll need a lot more than orthopaedic shoes in the future; she'll need a wheelchair to get around.

I sold the chiropody clinic. I got a great price for it. I have decided to go back to education. Dentistry this time. I am highly intelligent, and I am no fool. I am a quick learner. In a year or two I could have a nice little practice. No staff this time, I'll do it all myself.

It's funny, I started out working with anuses, then feet, and now I'm moving into oral. I have also found a new love for feet again. Not feet that smell like gorgonzola or wet skunk. Not ugly feet. Sexy feet. Feet in high heels and black stockings. TikTok plays a great part in this newly discovered eroticism.

THE PANTO

It's always the worst panto in the world. Every year without fail. So bad it's become a must see. A complete train wreck of a show. No talent involved whatsoever. The laughter from the audience is uncontrollable. The tickets fly out the door, the 3 shows are booked out almost immediately.

"It proves how bloody good we are," says Fr. Dominic, the director. He's been in charge of every show for the past 40 years. A weird looking man with a crooked left arm and a slight Richard III hump. "I love to hear laughter," he says. "I call it Vitamin L, what an essential part of our spiritual diet it is." Every Christmas a new show is put on in the church hall.

The acting troupe is small: the same 6 or 7 pensioners that have been together since the very beginning. Fr. Dominic always plays the Dame, no matter what the play. "It's very therapeutic and liberating in drag; the frock allows my creative juices to flow, and allows me relax in the character" he says. The odd actor or actresses may change over time due to death or invalidity. They call themselves *The Performing Pensioners.* If a good actor joins the group, they leave after a few days; they've a reputation to think of and do not want to be part of the insanity.

The panto this year is SNOW WHITE AND THE 7TH DWARF. Since Billy is the smallest, he got the part of the dwarf.
"Won't people be looking for the other 6 dwarfs," he asked Fr. Dominic, the director.
"Not in this production," the priest told him, "in this new reinvention the other 6 dwarfs are all dead; this is a follow-up to the original story. Madge will play Snow White, as she's the youngest at 69, and will be absolutely marvellous in my much improved upon version."
"Am I small enough?" asked Billy, still not feeling right for the part. He wasn't a tall man, but he wasn't a dwarf either.
"Absolutely," Fr. Dominic reassured him. "It's all about perspective. I'll keep you way upstage, it'll work out beautifully" And I'll put you in a school uniform, you'll look utterly wonderful, darling!"

Last year Rita, age 76, played the lead in Rapunzel. She had no hair, because of a bad case of alopecia, and had to join old wigs together with some gaffer tape. She also had dementia and often forgot what play she was in (one of the nights she turned into a different character half way through). The audience lapped it up. They loved it. She's not in this production as she is in a home for the bewildered now.

Fr. Dominic has aspirations of being a great Actor/Director. He sees himself as a Laurence Olivier or a John Gielgud. The locals call him 'The Holy Fool'. He lost interest in praying and other church stuff years ago. On Sunday his mass is the quickest you will ever attend. His heart isn't in it anymore. The only bit he still likes is the dressing up and the drinking of the alter wine. He buys the expensive bottles. "Jesus Christ deserves only the best plonk there is," he has said many a time.

The shows they put on are often inappropriate and offensive. Drag queens, queer jokes, and black face; they've done it all. And badly. But always to packed houses. "The most disgusting, debauched, degenerate and deranged so-called family entertainment I have ever had the displeasure to sit through," remarked the local school teacher. The boys and girls that went said it was "the absolute and best school trip in the world EVER".

SNOW WHITE AND THE 7TH DWARF went on after one week of rehearsals. "I don't like to over rehearse, it can spoil the spontaneity and the magic of the moment," Fr. Dominic says. He wrote a new prologue for his new production. The panto began with Snow White standing over 6 cardboard headstones (it was supposed to be 6 small coffins but that was too expensive). The stage was in darkness except for a spotlight over Snow White. The director was going for the Blessed Virgin with a halo effect. She read what was on each headstone; sobbing, and blessing herself in front of each of them.

        SNEEZY – RIP: Influenza
        BASHFUL – RIP: Nervous Breakdown
        SLEEPY – RIP: Narcolepsy
        HAPPY – RIP: Heart attack
        GRUMPY – RIP: Suicide
        DOC – RIP: Long-term Covid

The audience took part in a sing-a-long of Our Father and Hail Mary. Then DOEPY came on singing Heigh-ho, Heigh ho! He looked taller than Snow White. The perspective idea didn't seem to work. The show went downhill from there. The Evil Queen was played by Fr. Dominic. To be fair he looked a lot sexier than Rita. Old Rita was well past her sell-by date, and no amount of makeup or creative lighting could hide the fact. The poor woman resembled a mummified corpse.

The show then ended with a newly written epilogue.
The stage turned into what was meant to look like Heaven. (Fluffy clouds and a ladder reaching up into the rafters were added for the effect.) A voiceover of God was heard. The voice was recorded by Dermot, an actor who recently joined the group; he was a retired jam maker with plenty of time on his hands. "Never bloody again!" he said. "What a fiasco! I sound nothing like God - I'm a falsetto. I sound more like Willo the fuckin' Wisp!"

VOICE OF GOD

All SEVEN DWARFS are together once more. They live here in eternal peace with Snow White. I, God, watch over and look out for all of them up here. I've a special place in my kingdom for imps, goblins, leprechauns, gnomes, pixies, midgets, and even trolls. All people of stunted growth are welcome here. I grant them everlasting happiness. For I am the Almighty, and I created them in my image___

Heigh-ho, heigh-ho
Heigh-ho, heigh-ho, heigh-ho
Happy up in Heaven we are
Safe from down-below___

Then all the old actors took their bows. Snow White was exhausted, and had to be brought out in a wheelchair. Billy, the Dwarf, was mortified and stayed way upstage. Fr. Dominic, dressed as the Wicked Queen, did a solo number before blessing the entire congregation. The crowd was ecstatic, almost to the point of overexcitement.

SNOW WHITE AND THE 7TH DWARF was a complete failure. Meaning, it was a complete success. It was beyond hilarious. The laughter was non-stop, and hysterical. Not a dry seat in the house. Menopausal women lost control of their bladders; and grown men cried like babies throughout the show. The laughter continued all the way home.

Fr. Dominic is now planning a new panto for the Easter holiday: THE CRUSIFICTION ON ICE – A MUSICAL EXTRAVAGANA! A bigger budget this time. Laser beams and smoke machines. "I can't wait, it'll be an amazing no-expense-spared experience," he said, "early booking is advised."

And if they all work hard and nobody dies, or needs a hip replacement, and if they rehearse for more than just 1 week, they may just nail it.

THE DOUBLE ACT

Before Fanny and Lorrie took over driving the bus Jimmy was the driver. A man so skinny that one day he fell in between the back of the seat and wasn't found until Monday morning. He had smothered to death. Nobody knows how Fanny and Lorrie met; they have just always been together. A proper double act. One funny, one not so funny. They're the exact same as each other, except for their height, shape, personality and looks. They drive the bus now and deliver the meals-on-wheels in the area.

They have a system. One-day Fanny will work a little bit and Lorrie will do very little; and the next day Lorrie will work a little bit and Fanny will do very little. It's a one-person job really, but they are a double act and cannot be separated. A buy one - get one free - sort of deal. It's like they're invisibly joined at the hip. They even laugh the same way; it's irritating and annoying.

They got transferred here from the homeless shelter in Ballynoggin. It was closed down after a family of rats was found living in a sack of flour. The place was run by an eighty-year-old nun who ran it her way. "I work for Our Lord, Jesus Christ," she'd say, "and nobody else is going to tell me what to do." She was an uptight religious power-mad old witch. "Well, you'd better die real soon and get a cooking job up in heaven," the health officer told her as he handed her the closure order, "cause down here in the real world, I'm head honcho."

Fanny and Lorrie work in a new centre with a man from Madagascar who helps cook the food and clean the toilets. He's a good worker. Or at least he was a good worker until somebody back home put a spell on him. Now he just walks around saying "I'm going to die real soon, unless I can pay a lot of money to get this curse lifted!" Some dumb voodoo shit like this. In the right light he could be looked on as attractive; he wears an overpowering aftershave - or aphrodisiac - that attracts women to him like flies. Except his wife. She's had enough of him, "It was a badly arranged marriage," she said, "I hope the curse kills the bastard now!"

When Fanny or Lorrie have a day off it's a nightmare. It's as if an invisible umbilical cord has been cut. Separation anxiety takes hold (and the one left behind will need to be wrapped up in a blanket and given a hot mug of sweet tea). They are so close they finish each other's sentences. One will say, "Not a bad day," and the other will say, "as long as it doesn't rain." And other boring things. They even go to the toilet together. One of them has epilepsy - and the other one spasms and froths at the mouth. Onetime they had the same erotic dream, but only one of them had the orgasm. Jealousy is not rare between them.

Last year Fanny went on holiday, by herself, and came back with a facelift and a tummy tuck. She didn't look any younger or any thinner; she just looked different. After a few weeks the facelift and tummy tuck disappeared and she went back to her normal self. Lorrie was disgusted that she was left behind. "Do you not see that I need a facelift and a belly reduction just as much as you do," she told Fanny; "you're a selfish bitch, you should've took me with you."

There's a rumour going around that they both share the same husband. One has him Monday, Tuesday and Wednesday; and the other has him Thursday, Friday and Saturday (they give him Sunday off to rest). They live next door to each other, and neighbours have spotted a weird looking man climbing through their bedroom window in the dark of night. His name is Dick. He's a bin-man during the day and a taxi man at night. He clearly likes to double up. His cab always smells of rotten cabbages. Some say he's the first cousin to one of them and a half-brother to the other.

The centre Fanny and Lorrie work in has one other worker: a security man called Bob. His job is to open up in the morning and to close in the evening. He fails at this job. He calls himself a functioning alcoholic; he forgets to add: gambler and degenerate dope addict. He's intelligent, but he hides it very well. "Who's watching the watchers," he likes to say; and "I get paid for doin' fuck all - I'll never work again!" Security is needed. It's a rough neighbourhood. Vandalism and arson are the chosen hobbies of the youths in the area. Bob never has money for food or other luxuries - he spends it all on the horses, weed and booze. Fanny and Lorrie throw him a takeaway meal most days.

The meals are cheap. They are also crap. Not one of them can cook. If it doesn't come out of a tin, or can be put in a microwave, they don't know what to do. Actually, once they did put a tin in the microwave and nearly blew up the building. The meals keep the local pensioners and homeless out of the health system for a bit longer. A stop-gap; before they end up on a hospital trolley or in the hospice or in the morgue.

Fanny and Lorrie are so like-minded - if you have a row with one of them - the other one will also hold the grudge. Each morning one has to kick-start, motivate the other one, or nothing will get done - but today, Lorrie actually kicked Fanny in the stomach, and knocked her glasses off with a smack. She was always a little more dominant; always had a bit more confidence and self-esteem. People call them the Lion and the Pussycat or Tweedledee and Tweedledum.

They are not friends anymore.
Maybe they were never friends; maybe they just grow up together, became too close. It's believed onetime they had more than a platonic relationship (they've been seen blushing and touching each other in the kitchen). The kick to the stomach and the smack to the face has ended the relationship between them. Some say Fanny was pregnant - and that's why Lorrie kicked her in the stomach. Others say it was because one of them got a pay rise and the other didn't.

They hate each other now.
They'll no longer work as a team. The double act has officially split up. "We used to be two peas in a pod," said one of them, "now we're like chalk and fuckin' cheese," the other one shouted from the far end of the kitchen.

THE STATE OF THE ART
PURPOSELY BUILT NURSING HOME

Most of the OAP's sit in their en-suite rooms all day, in their nightgowns or PJ's, watching reruns of Murder She Wrote and Magnum PI, on their flat-screen TV's. But a few of them are not as doddery, or as senile, and want more. They want to cling on to that semblance and imagination of power; they want to hold on to that VIP status – they have high IQ's and do not like to be treated like invalids or idiots.

This small group has set up a Board of Directors. There is no business, or company, they just merely set up a Board of Directors so they can be in charge of something. Anything was better than sitting around all day and waiting for death.

The Board consists of Maude, William, Mavis, and Derek - the CEO. They meet at 3PM every day in the chapel on the 4nd floor. They're allowed to run the meetings without any interference from the real world. (There's also a sleeping partner, but he suffers from narcolepsy, and wouldn't even be trusted to turn up for an AGM.) "They couldn't organise a piss-up in a brewery," one member of staff said to another, "or a wank in a brothel," the other one laughed, as he emptied the bedpan. The staff is young and spend most of their time on their phones - messaging each other things like LOL, WTF & OMG. "I'm paid minimum wage; it's a dead-end job here, not a calling or a vocation!" one of them said.

Most of the residents have dementia. They do not even know what day of the week it is - and that's why their pensions go directly to the nursing home (usually their houses are sold and the money is handed over before admission.) The philosophy of the state of the art purposely built nursing home is: TLC. And to provide a living environment that mirrors the previous lifestyle (as much as possible). To ensure the residents live in a comfortable and clean and safe environment; maintaining their independence (as far as possible).

There are beautiful landscaped gardens. Ducks and frogs and squirrels can be seen. There is also a pond and picnic tables and hammocks. If the weather is good the residents are allowed sit outside and sunbathe; sometimes even a bed will be wheeled out with one of the less mobile residents. They used to have wonderful BBQ's until one old person choked to death on a skewer. 'Eileen Ryan: R.I.P' is now engraved on a small plaque on a bench.

Inside the complex everything is new and modern. There are vending machines on each floor (selling incontinent pads and Dentifix). There's also an ICU and an A&E ward in the basement. And a small crematorium is situated at the far end of the garden. The Luxury Home is expensive. All the old folks had good jobs in their previous lives, or are lucky enough to have wealthy sons and daughters.

The award-winning complex has a huge kitchen, with a real chef. Perfectly chosen food is prepared every day. For starters there is a hot broth or Bovril. The main course will consist of mashed potatoes, gravy, or some kind of sauce. The desserts are rice pudding, custard, semolina and tapioca, served with strawberry jam. Jelly & ice-cream will be served on special occasions. There is no shortage of concentrated prune juice. And if any of the residents have a problem eating, that's OK, the option of squashed, blended, purred and liquidized food is available.

A bell rings for mealtime and for bedtime. They are two different sounding bells; but still some residents get confused and end up getting into bed instead of going to the dining room, and vice versa. Last week an old couple escaped, went AWOL. Eventually they were found trying to dock a cruise ship together. After they were returned, all the door and lift codes were changed, and ID cards were hung around their necks. A strict observation and segregation of the sexes is now being talked about.

"Today we will prepare a letter of our discontent," said Derek, the CEO, "enough is enough!" Maude, William and Mavis also attended the meeting in the chapel. Maeve took the minutes, as she had the best hearing and handwriting of the lot of them. Sometimes if the board meeting went on too long, a staff member would bring in some tea and ginger nuts. But this is not encouraged by the matron, "They've only had their dinner and their nap, let's not spoil their appetite just before teatime."

"This place is nothing but a glorified prison," said William, "they take our money, and they leave us here to rot." He's a big man with IBS and an enlarged prostate. He used to be a banker for AIB. He lived life to the full, drove a 190MPH soft-top BMW. Now he's squeezed into a motorised wheelchair with a top speed of 5MPH. He suffers from flatulence and BO. Everybody tries to keep upwind of him.

"And the food here is awful," complained Mavis, "I'm sick of the muck they keep feeding us." She looked out the chapel window, and continued, "I'd like to see frog's legs and some duck a l'orange on the menu for a change!"

"At least some KFC," interjected Maude, as she clipped her toenails under the table.

They wrote a list of demands

1. Access to the Porn Channel (not just BBC1, UTV, HBO and NBC).
2. A weakly pocket money allowance.
3. Shorter family visits.
4. Vending machines to stock Red Bull, condoms, and bags of peanut M&M's.
5. A football, or boxing club, to replace the knitting and the bingo.

The letter ended P.S.

We better hear back from you ASAP - or you will have a lock-in and a dirty protest on your hands!

The Board of Directors

THE RAPID WEIGHT LOSS WEEKEND

I run rapid weight loss weekends. They're somewhat controversial (I like to call them, breakthrough) and not for everybody. But they work. I don't over charge either; they're as cheap as chips to join. I don't like to label or classify people. I don't care if they're overweight, or morbidly obese - I simply lump them all together as, Fat.

I'm what you'd call a myth buster, a teller of truths. A lot of stuff others tell you is bullshit and lies. I've one motto I live by: THE MOUTH HOLE IS BIGGER THAN THE BUTT HOLE. Simple isn't it? Eat less; lose more. I offer people an intense three-day weight loss camp. When they leave, they'll have lost a shit load of weight. And that's a fact. And they get to take home all that wisdom I've thought them.

I'm not naturally skinny myself. I'm more of an elephant or rhinoceros, than a giraffe or gazelle; but I work hard to look the part I need to look. I'm unhealthy, but I look good. When I was fat I felt great; all warm and cosy. Now I'm always cold and miserable. I'm good at what I do. The proof is in the pudding. Happy customers every time. I see myself more as a psychologist than a dietician. An inspirational quote I use: Just because you're overweight, doesn't mean you can't be as happy as a pig in shite.

I'm originally from the inner city. As rough as fuck a place to grow up. It was worse than dog eat dog. It was you stab me, I shoot you, sort of place. RATS OUT and JOXER'S A SCUMBAG written on every wall. I was lucky to get out. I spent a few years in jail. (It's none of your damn business.) That's where I learned the art of cooking slop on a budget. A few years later I got lucky - my husband fell down a manhole in work and he died. Somebody left the lid off. I got a big compensation. And bought this house down here in the arsehole of nowhere. Some people call me vulgar, but I don't give a shit about that.

The fat people come and stay here in my house. I knocked the four bedrooms I had into one big dormitory. Now I can fit twelve or fourteen of them, at a squeeze. Bunk beds with army blankets. Comfort is not important. Losing the weight is important. They arrive at five o' clock on the Friday. I show them around and give them a quick run-through of the rules. Then they get supper. Two slices of toast with flora margarine and black tea. The choice is, take it or leave it. Most of them won't take it. Then it's off for a three-hour aerobic workout before bed.

I wake them up at 6 o' clock. Breakfast is gruel with dried prunes. They can have as much instant black coffee as they want. Caffeine is good (it keeps them moving and not blocked up). I don't care if they smoke (it's an easy way to keep the weight off). Then it's out into the field with them. The house came with a lot of land. All very neglected and overgrown. Digging, weeding, and chopping down trees is the perfect way to knock some flab off. I let them have water whenever they want (except on the last day - it can cause fluid retention and give a false reading at the weigh-in).

A simple trick I use is to cook degusting and horrible food. And to give fuck all selection. If the food looks unappealing and unappetising chances are they won't want it. That means I don't have to buy loads of groceries. Lunch is scrambled egg whites and one Ryvita biscuit. Again half of them won't want it. You see, already the weight's falling off. I'm not here to make them happy - I'm here to knock the fat off them.

If it's raining out they'll spend most of their time on the treadmills. Sometimes I have to tie their hands to the rails with cable ties. It's all done out of kindness and to achieve the end goal. They might be angry at the time, but by Monday, they're a lot happier with their new shape. The aim is weight loss. Am I wrong? I like to keep them active at all times.

As I said, I'm a myth breaker. For example: candyfloss in no way bad for you. (It may rot your teeth, but that's not my concern, I'm not a dentist.) In fact, it's ok to eat loads of it. It weighs nothing. Am I wrong? I knew a woman who survived only eating cotton wool balls until she died. Some of my clients like to wrench and puke. That's very normal. I encourage it. But I'll give them their own a mop and bucket to clean up after themselves.

Believe it or not, Anorexia, Bulimia, Cancer and Aids - are all great ways of keeping weight off. But they're looked on as a bit dramatic. Also I'm not able to take any credit for the weight lost. Some even come here with elastic bands tied around their bowels. These people need very little help from me. I'll just let them to do a light bit of gardening over the weekend. And for the ones with more money than sense, I have my diet pills, or placebos, for sale.

I want to bring out a cookbook.
It wouldn't be for everyone. But it would be very successful. My idea is to turn people off eating. They call me mad, but it makes perfect sense to me. Food is always made look and taste too good. That's the problem. That's why the world's so full of fat people. A local publisher said he'd consider printing it. But only if I make the recipes more appealing and tone down the bad language.
'Fuck off!' I told him. 'You can take the woman outa the inner-city; but you can't take the inner-city outa the woman!'
This leopard won't change her spots for anybody.

The book won't be full of glossy pictures of gorgeous looking food. It'll be straight to the point. Recipes that make you not want to eat; that might even make you sick.
Eat less, lose weight, keep moving - that's my philosophy. A motivational quote I like to use is: Shut up, and lower your goddamn expectations. And, of course, don't forget: THE MOUTH HOLE IS BIGGER THAN THE BUTT HOLE.

Here are a few of my recipes.

SORBET

1 lemon
2 tablespoons of cat's piss
Scrapped ice from the freezer door

Put in a glass and fuck at the wall

MAYONNAISE

3 yolks of salmonella hen's period
Splatter of engine oil

First, fuck the sperm-like part down the sink
Then, beat the shit out of the rest
(Make sure to book a GP appointment)

SPAGHETTI BOLOGNESE

Some cheap minced dead cow
Garlic powder
Squirt of tomato ketchup
Pasta

Eat the pasta raw (al dente)
And fuck the rest down the toilet
(Cut out the middleman)

CODLE

8 cocktail size penises
6oz of pig grizzle
Water
Leftover vegetables

Fling it all into a pot
Boil until a scum forms
Give it to the dog

QUICK 'N' EASY BBQ

Buy a load of cheap out of date meat
(generally covered in spicy sauce by
the butcher to hide the gone-off
look and taste)

Pour petrol over it, and light
Then eat, and get pissed
(Have bedpan handy)

CHICKEN CURRY IN A HURRY

2 oversized chopped chicken breasts
(pumped with hormones and nipples removed)
A heap of extra hot curry powder
1 large onion (Optional)

Don't bother to peel the onion,
just fuck it in the pot
Add rice (leftover from your grannies
Sunday pudding – remember to
remove the jam and skin)

A twin pack of kitten-soft toilet rolls
(Non-optional)

BREAKFAST FOR A HEALTHY BOWEL

Grab any box of overpriced cereal
Fuck contents in bin
Eat box
Done

PLAYS & MONOLOGUES

The Undertaker Bros. and *The Dentist* are part of, with some changes, the full length play, **Comedy of Horrors.**

The Recluse, The Burn Victim, The Alcoholic, and *The Toilet Cleaner,* are all part of the play **Nuthouse.**

The Happy Death of Reggie Crumb is a shortened version of the play, **Crabtree's Last Stand.**

The Undertaker Bros.   63

The Recluse   77

The Happy Death of Reggie Crumb   80

The Burn Victim   85

The Alcoholic   87

The Toilet Cleaner   91

The Dentist   93

THE UNDERTAKER BROS.

Celebrating 100 Years of Dying

CHARACTERS

Donald *and* ***Fred*** *Black are Undertakers. They are brothers and live together above the family shop.*

The two men are in their nightclothes, at a table, playing a game of draughts. Donald hasn't got his mind on the game; Fred is becoming impatient.

FRED

>It's your move.

DONALD

>Patience, Fred. This isn't like chess. It takes a lot of strategy. *(He is constantly sneaking something from his pocket and nibbling it)*

FRED

>What are you doin'?

DONALD

>*(Defensive)* Nothing!

FRED

>Just take a move will you! *(Donald takes a move they play the game)* What are you doin'? You're eatin' something!

DONALD

> I'm not! *(Takes something out of his pocket)* It's only a few crackers!

FRED

> You're either eatin' or you're not eatin! Nibbling like a bloody hamster! *(He gets up from the table)* It's raining again.

DONALD

> Is it?

FRED

> It's always bloody raining.

DONALD

> It is, isn't it.

FRED

> I got to keep a couple more of them coffins. Good ones they are too.

DONALD

> We're supposed be burning them Fred. I don't like it. It's not right. The families paid for them.

FRED

> Shite! It's only the odd one we get to keep. A little perk. *(Pause)* You've no idea what some of them families are like. Hangin' around after the cremation. They watch everything. *(Pause)* It's such a waste. Burnin' up all our profits.

DONALD

> Do you know what I can't understand, Fred? *(He continues eating)*

FRED

> *(After a long wait)* What *can't* you understand, Donald?

DONALD

> How people like this whole cremation thing. In and out and it's all over. Where's the respect in that? People used to like to look at the coffin goin' into the ground. Standing around in the rain. Throwing the bit of muck on. That's all part of it. The grieving process. It's too easy just burning someone. There's no skill, no art in that. *(Pause)* And stop skimping on the wood as well. That last coffin was very small. I had to make the body fit.

FRED

> Donald! I'm not getting through to you. We have to start thinking profit. This business is a going concern. We need to see an increase in our profit margin. Next year is a very important year for us___

DONALD

> Profit! Profit my backside! Everything's not about making money, Fred. *(Pause)* The old ways are always best. People like the whole funeral thing. The ceremony. It's a day out. Tradition, Fred. It's all about tradition. Do you not understand that?

FRED

> What's wrong with up-grading a bit. We can do a hell of a lot more cremations in a week than we can funerals. Time management. That's what we should be thinking. Forget digging holes; you can get two bodies into one of them cavity blocks, then cover it over with a bit of a plaque!

DONALD

> Horrible! That's horrible, Fred. I don't want to know about it. Our father would be turning in his grave, if he heard you. *(Pause)* What happened to the craft of undertaking? All the stuff that's been handed down to us. Age old secrets. And I'm not just talking about our family, but right back to the Egyptians, the mummies. They knew a thing or two. *(Pause)* It's only a fad. People will always want the old ways.

FRED

> If you don't adapt, Donald, you die. Times are changing.

DONALD

> Why is next year a very important year for us, Donald?

FRED

> What year is next year, Fred? *(He doesn't wait for the answer)* Next year we are 100 years in the family funeral business, Donald!

DONALD

> No, Fred. This shop was opened in... *(He trys to think)* That makes it, *(He adds up on his fingers)* that will make it ... well, not 1oo years yet!

FRED

> Don't be thick! Nobody knows that! It's a centenary! 100 years! I even got flyers done up to prove it. *(He takes out some flyers to show Donald. He reads one)*

DONALD AND FRED BLACK

**The time-honoured
and traditional family
run undertakers**

**Burying the local community
for the PAST 100 years**

**To celebrate
we are giving away
free lining
with all our coffins**

DONALD

>But that's a lie, Donald! That's cheating.

FRED

>Shut up, Donald! Everybody does it!

DONALD

>I don't like it! *(Thinking)* Maybe it would be OK to commemorate, not celebrate, in a very small way. In a respectful way.

FRED

>Exactly! Celebrate/Commemorate! Tomayto/tomatho! What's the bloody difference!

DONALD

>*(Out of the blue)* I'm putting on the weight, Fred. I'm getting fat again.

FRED

>Here we go again! *(Pause)* Donald ... you are not fat!

DONALD

> *(Distressed)* I am. I'm disgusting. I've got fat legs. Fat fingers. Fat everything. *(He brings a weighing scales and gets on)* Look! Look! That's six ounces up on yesterday! I've got layers of skin everywhere. Folds of skin. My bum is hanging down in pleats!

FRED

> Stop it! Stop it, Donald. Listen to your brother. I'm telling you, you are not fat! You were fat once. But you are not fat now. A bit pudgy, that's all. *(Pause)* You always get like this; it's because we're not busy. People are living too long nowadays that's the problem. Our grandfather would've turned out forty, fifty coffins in a week. Now what? Lucky if it's five or six! In the good ol' days people knew how to die; they dropped like flies, they did. In the good ol' war years, the coffins in here were stacked up to the ceiling, they were.

DONALD

> I don't want to be busy, Fred. We don't need the money. We live up stairs. A couple of bodies for us to work on at a time is all we need. Profit is all you think about. You're getting greedy. And it's showing in your work.

FRED

> I just don't like waste, that's all. Half the stuff we do people don't even notice. The big co-ops, they take loads of short cuts. With their massive walk-in mortuaries. Bang, bang, bang. In and out, no messin' about. They rack up the bodies and knock out funerals like there's no tomorrow.

DONALD

> That's not what we are about here. We offer a small, personal service. We always did.

FRED

> Well, it's time to think bigger. We should open this place up a bit. Make a showroom out of it. We have to think outside the box. People want cheap and cheerful. People want cardboard coffins, and funny songs. It's the future. We need to attract younger people in here. Everybody that comes in here is so old.

DONALD

> Have more respect, Donald! The other day I heard you say to an old woman who was in mourning her dead husband, 'It's hardly worth your while going home!' You can't say that. It's inappropriate.

FRED

> We need to put the fun back in fun-erals, Fred!

DONALD

> Have you gone insane! May God forgive you!

FRED

> Oh, yeah, God - that reminds me. We need to get a Web page done up. It's all www dot now. Religion isn't the thing anymore. People are too informed. It's not God anymore, it's Google! *(...)* There's good business to be had out there. People have more money than sense nowadays. And we should take it from them *before* they die!

DONALD

> *(Not listening)* I'm just not happy, Fred. I *am* putting on weight. Anybody can see that. They look at me and they see the overweight undertaker. I can't even fit into one of our own coffins.

FRED

    Christ! I give up. Who cares what weight you are? Fat. Thin. Nobody cares.

DONALD

    I need to get out more. This place is getting me down. Everybody we meet is so serious. Crying all the time. *(Pause)* I'm sensitive. It's not good for me. Just because death runs in our family, we have to do it! We should've learnt when our grandfather fell into one of his own coffins, with a chisel in his hand, ending up staked like Dracula!

FRED

    No, don't! Stop it, Donald. *(Pause)* You're just depressed again. Depressed; and a bit pudgy. That's all. Snap out of it. I don't know what's wrong with you. We have a nice business; our own hours. Nobody to nag us, or tell us what to do___

DONALD

    I'm thinking of getting married Fred.

FRED

    (Shocked) What the hell brought this on? Who have you been talking to?

DONALD

    Nobody. I'd just like to try it.

FRED

    You're not thinking straight, Donald. You're just a bit down. I'll cook you something nice for supper. Some nice liver and onions.

DONALD

> No. I'm on a diet!

FRED

> Diet? What diet? You haven't refused a meal yet. You're always eating. I see you.

DONALD

> What do you mean always eating! *(Takes a biscuit from his pocket)* They're only crackers! No butter. No jam. Plain wafer thin crackers!

FRED

> You don't need a woman, Donald. Things are fine the way they are.

DONALD

> I feel like there's something missing. Every day is the same here. It would be nice to have a woman laughing around the place.

FRED

> What! Here! We don't need a woman here. We can laugh. I can laugh more. If that's what you want. *(Tries to make Donald laugh)* Did you hear the one about the fella who fell into a vat of varnish. A terrible end, but a beautiful finish! Or. What did the corpse say when they lowered his coffin into the wrong hole? 'You're making a grave mistake.' *(Donald is not impressed)* A *grave* mistake, Donald! Please yourself. I don't know why I bother! *(...)* Anyway, a woman wouldn't like it here, with all the dead bodies. The smell and everything. It would depress her. You'd depress her. You do that to people.

DONALD

> The job isn't enough for me, Fred. You're right - we do need changes around the place. Working on bodies all the time just makes me eat more. I need to get out and meet people. Yesterday when I was draining Mrs Crabshaw - she was a tough old bird, the rigor mortis had set in long before she died - all I could think of was fried chicken!

FRED

> Yeah, well, you have to eat. It's only natural. You're too hard on yourself. When I'm at a cremation sometimes, my minds not always there; I'm thinking about the lovely barbeque ribs we're going to have later. It's natural. Anyway you are not eating so much lately.

DONALD

> I sort of eat in bursts. Sneaky eating. *(He takes biscuits from another pocket and eats them)* It's a bit of a habit. The more unhappy I am, the more I eat. Everywhere I go there seems to be food hidden around the place.

FRED

> You are happy, Donald You only think you're not. I've seen you when you have finished working on one of them corpses. The proud look on your face.

DONALD

> That part I like. Yeah. Dressing the bodies. Putting the make-up on them, and all that. But I still feel there's something missing.

FRED

> What could be missing! You can drain and stuff a corpse like no man alive. When you're finished with them they look years younger. Like models, they look.

DONALD

> It's true. I am good. I know a few tricks. The way I can put putty behind the eyes to stop that sunken look; the way I fill-up all the orifices with cotton wool to stop any leakage and keep out the maggots; the stitching; the sewing. All self-thought. I can manipulate just about any face into looking like it's only having a nap. You have to be a hairdresser and everything. Restoration is an art form.

FRED

> True. You make dead bodies beautiful.

DONALD

> But ... I don't know Fred, maybe if I was married ... I would be happier.

FRED

> That doesn't make sense to me, Donald. That doesn't make any sense. Do you not remember Ma and Da. They were married. And would you have called them happy? They were miserable, they were. They hated each other___

DONALD

> *(Annoyed)* I won't have you talkin' about mam and dad like that!

FRED

> *(...)* Why don't you get yourself a dog? That would be good company. They're very loyal and obedient. They can be trained to do little tricks.

DONALD

> Don't be trying to annoy me, Fred! A dog is a terrible thing to happen to a person. That's all I need, to have to go around picking up another animals poo all day! Anyway, dogs don't live as long as people. When it dies I wouldn't know what to do. I'm an undertaker, not a taxidermist.

FRED

> Get yourself a cat. They have nine lives. Any type of pet at all will do. What about a little rabbit. When it dies you could make a stew out of it!

DONALD

> No. I want a woman.

FRED

> And who'd you get to go out with you? Everybody you meet is already dead. They're already dead, Donald.

DONALD

> Oh, you think you're so clever. What about all those wives that are left behind? They seem very unhappy. Maybe one of them would like me? *(Pause)* They'd be feeling a bit sad, need a bit of cheering up.

FRED

> *(Sarcastically)* What would you do? What would you say: 'I'm very sorry about your husband, would you like to come out for a meal with me!'

DONALD

> *(Excited)* Yeah. Why not. We could go somewhere swanky. Black tie. Limo. I'd get a big T-bone steak. Bottle of red wine. Roast and mashed potatoes. Pudding. The lot.

FRED

> Stop it Donald! STOP IT! *(He grabs Fred)* We don't need a woman here! Change is not good for you. You're not thinking straight.

DONALD

> Yeah. Yeah, you're right. Maybe I'll take it a little slower. *(Pause)* Show my respects first. Send along a wreath with the bill, or something. After all I've just embalmed the poor woman's husband. Don't want to move too fast. *(Pause)* Yes. A woman's touch. That's what this place needs. A bit of decoration. Brighten things up a bit. Maybe a nice bit of home baking. The smell of fresh bread around the place. *(Pause)* It would be nice if she liked her food too.

FRED

> *(Agitated)* We must think of our work, Donald. Undertaking comes first. The family business. It's all we know. We've two corpses in the freezer waiting for hygienic treatment. *(Pause)* We need each other. It's just you and me Donald___

DONALD

> *(Not listening)* A woman of my own. And she'd need me. Her husband would be only just dead. *(Pause)* We could have breakfast in bed together: smoked kippers ... garlic french bread ... flap-jacks ... Oh! I feel good. All I want to do is eat!
>
> *(He takes a tin with fancy cakes in it from under the table)* To hell with it! *(Stuffs a cake into his mouth)* Let the flesh pile on, let buttons pop! I've decided to get married Fred! I'm gonna get.......

(Fred loses control. He strangles and kills Donald in the chair)

FRED

It's you and me, Donald. We'll have no more talk of bringin' some silly woman in here to disturb our peace. You were right - the old ways are best ... who needs changin' things that don't need fixin' ... all this talk about burning being the new thing; it's only cheapening what has been an important legacy handed down to us by our forefathers. We'll keep things the way they always were. *(...)* We can hold off on the 100 year celebrations. *(...)* Bringing some woman into our home wouldn't be right, Donald. It wouldn't be right. She'd start meddling; not happy with anything ... before long she'd want rid of me, Donald; gettin' in her way and all. She'd change everything! *(Pause)* It's just you and me, Donald ... just you and me. No big changes for us ... a little compromise maybe, but that's to be expected ... *(...)* It's your move, Donald. It's your move. *(Lights fade)*

THE RECLUSE

A monologue

Emily Thorndike is well educated, morose, and in constant pain.

The play is set in the past. An old style bed, invalid chair etc. It opens with a piece of classical music.

A light shows us Emily Thorndike in bed/chair. She talks to the audience. The light fades in and out, with confusion of time.

EMILY

The wild cherry trees in my garden are tame and no longer bear fruit. Everything is overgrown and undernourished. It is a bitter new morning. The daylight is persistent in its shinning. I never much liked the sun. That is not to say that I like the rain; but I do so very much like the snow. I am rambling now. The doctor said that that would happen. He was here to hear my chest this this morning. I do not like the way he touches me. 'All is, as all should be,' he tells me. Philistine. An invisible disease is visibly killing me. I hate what I cannot see.

I have not left this bed for such a long time. I do not think I ever shall. Everything is brought to me by Mildred. *(Pause)* I am still very constipated. Damn Doctors! They are trying to finish me. They give me things to help me sleep. This is all I seem to do now. I wish Mildred would turn that damn sun down. She is keeping me alive on purpose. I will *never* forgive her for that.

I am still very constipated. And have a bed rash. Sitting here crooked and twisted I see nothing but a wasted and unwanted life. An existence that was all wrong for me. The problem is: I got what I so very much wanted. And now it is destroying me - from the inside out. *(Calls out)* Mildred! ... Mildred! Where is that girl?

The pain in my body is immense and unrelenting. I have not been the same since the last stroke. Today I have a birthday. I am filled with nothing but regrets. It was not always so. I loved a young man once. So handsome, and kind. We had such plans. *(Pause)* The past is past. And not much of a past it is at present.

(Showing bandages) I sliced my wrists today. Not to die. Just to let some of the pain out. The doctor scolded me. He bandaged my arms. Then gave me a sedative. If I had died, what would they have said: 'Unrequited love?' 'Mental illness?' 'Crushed hopes?' Indeed, it may have been that the motive lay in all, or none of these directions.

I told Mildred to go and collect some chestnuts, or milk some hens or something. *(Pause)* Thomas was my whole world. I had no feeling, *except* for his love. *(Pause)* Only when he was gone, did I truly feel the utter emptiness. It was as if the sky fell around my ankles. *(Pause)* How could he have left me in such a vulnerable state? He knew of the sickness that could take hold, and smother me.

It was in the sanatorium that I wrote him not to return. My brain was so distorted and muddled. Such love I felt could not last. He sent many letters pleading for my change of heart. In time he stopped writing.

A clergyman once told me: 'That satisfaction of the flesh was evil, a sin'. He said, 'Genuine love was not a feeling of pleasure, or lust. It should, rather - be a sacrifice. He said, 'One must find the fulfilment of life in its violent and cruel struggles; in the cleansing and searching of the soul'. *(Pause)* I never forgot that. *(Pause)* I made a mistake. *(Pause)* My fate has been my punishment.

This coffin of a bed has made me lose track of time. There were two cats outside my window today. Mildred has been feeding them. I am in a state of confusion. If only I could control my thoughts. They steam through my head like a locomotive.

If in life, there had only been a map. A correct path to choose. I feel I am going insane. Like a little raw creature with the skin peeled away, the naked bones visible. *(She picks up a looking glass)* I have been a coward. Fear and doubt are all that remain. *(Pause)* I cannot look in the mirror without reflecting on my ill judgments, my mistakes.

I do not belong to the future. It is, is it not, a matter of quality versus quantity! Oh! Not to think, I think, is the only answer. And death, the only cure.

I have drawn up my will. I want this to be the end. The body will have to be disposed of. All the usual rituals and conventions shall have to been seen to. I find myself praying. I do not like it.

I have no soul. It left my body long ago. My once beautiful garden is now dead and full of weeds. I see no future. Only a row of headstones. Graves of neglect. Not memories to respect. I have soiled the bed again. Oh! Enough. Enough! Let the snow fall and cover this imperfect world. (*Lights down*)

THE HAPPY DEATH OF
REGGIE CRUMB

SCENE: *A small, dirty room.*

REGGIE: *Is unshaven, sitting at a typewriter. He wears a soiled dressing gown over old pyjamas. He has glasses, and is unwell looking.*

BILLY: *Enters carrying a suitcase. He looks sharp in a new suit. He is confident, with a slight American accent.*

NOTE: REGGIE *and* BILLY *never talk to each other; their monologues are delivered to the audience. (They exist in their own space.) A light comes on over the actor who is speaking; the other actor is in semi-darkness (but does not necessarily have to remain still).*

REGGIE *sits at an old typewriter. He is surrounded by books.* BILLY *enters with his hall-door keys in his hand. A light comes on over him. He puts down his suitcase. Surveys the room. He pays no attention to his brother.*

BILLY

> This place hasn't changed much. It's still a dump. Dry and wet rot. An example of bloody poverty. To think I had to grow up in this. No wonder I had all them chest infections. Always sick I was. Force-fed cod liver oil and liver salts. It's amazing I got this far. The best thing I ever did was leave. I wasn't gonna stay and just exist in this poverty-stricken pigsty. *(Light off)*

REGGIE

> *(Light comes on over him)* Bleedin' Billy was lucky to get out when he did. Skippin' off to America. The little opportunist. All silly skyscrapers and rotten big apples. Oh, the busy businessman. Never one postcard. Not even a mass card! *(Coughing, drinking whisky)* I don't get much invited to people's houses anymore. Not since ma died. People rather me not around.

BILLY

>   *(Looking around)* Why the hell anyone would want to stay here is beyond me! I suppose some families like to stay together. The huddled mass. No get-up-and-bloody-go in the lot of them. Never wanting to move on. Make some decent money. Better themselves. *(Takes out a gold cigarette case and lighter)* I must've fuckin' been adopted. The only one in the family with ambition. Take a leaf outa my book. You want to get somewhere in life? WORK WORK WORK - that's what it's all about! Let nothin' or no one stand in your way. It's about survival. The fittest. The desire to succeed. I've made more money in one year, than they all had in their whole goddamn lifetime. *(He smokes)*

REGGIE

>   *(Mockingly)* WORK WORK WORK - that's what it's all about! WRITE WRITE WRITE - that's what it's all about! *(Hitting the typewriter keys)* Hammering the words onto the page. Sweat and blood. Havin' somethin' to say. *(Pause)* Our Billy knew nothing. He was always a fool. *(Coughing, bringing up phlegm into a handkerchief)* TB. Or not TB. *(Still coughing)* That is congestion!

BILLY

>   I'm looked up to. Respected in the community. *(Walking around, blowing dust off things)* Paying off a fine big house. Four bedrooms. When me and the little wife have a fight, I have a choice in which room to sleep in. *(He gives a stupid laugh)* Every so often we invite people over. *(Stops and thinks)* Ma would've loved to visit. She was always on about it. Can you imagine her in her hairnet and yellow rubber gloves? *(Pause)* The journey would've been too much for her. *(Pause)* Oh, yeah, things are good. I have the very best of everything. Everything I hoped for. My life's on track. It's a good life.

REGGIE

A load of shite. That's all it is. You've got to be smart; you got to write yourself out of it. Our Billy never wrote. Looked at books with pictures in them. Under his bed, dirty filthy little magazines. That's all he cared about. *(Pause)* He could have any girl he wanted. Mr. Perfect in his perfect world. *(Thinking)* It was harder for me. A freak, a face full of acne. Acne and boils. It had to be both! A bit chubby. A sissy, 'cause I was no good at football. I'm glad I was never picked. I never wanted to be in their stupid games, anyway. All of them in some sort of gang. Swappin' their fleas and snot-filled sandwiches. Beating each other up after school. *(Pause)* Billy was in their gang, alright. He did whatever he had to, to be liked.

(Thinking fondly) There was one girl he used to bring home. When he was still in school. A pale little thing. Mousy brown hair. She was lovely. She used to sit and talk to me in the kitchen. Really quite. With little round glasses. And she read. She read loads. Then Billy dumped her. *(Pause)* She never came around after that.

BILLY

You think I'd have all that if I stayed here? This place was the no-hope express. Goin' nowhere. *(Pause)* Ma never looked for much more. She was the type that was content to just have a husband. Be a wife. Have a kippy house to clean. A couple of kids to nag. She was a hard aul woman. Rigid. Happy, to be unhappy - that's how I'd put it. Always sewing communion dresses, or something. She might as well have been stitchin' fuckin' mailbags. We weren't goin' anywhere. She never had two shillings to rub together. Her idea of a family day out was to bring us to the graveyard. Can you imagine that? *(Pause)* Dad always did his own thing. Never saw much of him. He loved his drink, though. She probably drove him to it.

REGGIE

> The aul fella worked catching rats in the Corporation long before I did. He had the face of a rat; the body of a weasel; and the personality of a parasite. He gave mother an awful time. He'd make her feel unattractive with his sheepish stares lookin' at all those younger, thinner lookin' women. He ignored me. I was invisible. *(Pause)* They never talked to each other much; just fought all the time. Never once saw him smile. Or heard him laugh. Maybe in the pub with all his cronies, his admirers. It upset mother a lot. His indiscretions. His little infidelities. *(...)* She'd be lucky to get any wage outa him. I'd rob his pockets when he'd fall down drunk. Piss-stained stupid. We'd put him to bed. I'd stand there lookin' at him. Listenin' to him snorin'. Staring at his false teeth in the glass. *(...)* He was found sitting on the loo bleeding to death. A gut full of stout. And a pocket full of betting slips. Not much of a life was it. To exist, and then just die.

BILLY

> You'd think Reggie, been the older brother, would've been strong enough to get out. In his own world, he was. Hiding in his room. With his so-called problems. Read read read like a bloody worm. Bed sores and brain damage. No wonder he had milk bottles for glasses. Da gets him a real job in the Corporation. And still he writes them silly stories. What's so clever about writers, anyway? Havin' to make stuff up.

REGGIE

> *(Annoyed)* A REAL job! With a herd of poxy morons! Drink pissy tea. Read the sports page. Get through the day; run for the clock-card. Straight to the pub. The same stupid jokes. The same macho bullshit. Pretend to like each other. Plastic People. Carbon Copy Shit Heads! *(Pause)* I'm glad they got rid of me.

BILLY

> I was always stronger than he was. He was weak. Happy to stay at the bottom of the ladder. Nothing like me. Not that I was smart. I was a bit thick, to be honest. The only thing the Christian Brothers ever thought me was how to duck a good bleedin' hidin'! Reggie had the brains to burn. But as I always say: there's smart, and there's smart! Never used his brains the way he was supposed to. *(Pause)* He definitely had a screw or two missin' to stay in this hole. *(Pause)* It's a very big world out there. *(Pause)* I had to get out. Could he not see that? Why couldn't he see that? (*Exits*)

REGGIE

> It was mother and me that kept things goin'. The house spick and span. She was obsessed by it. Every room. Every floor. Every speck of dust. (*Showing actions*) Wipe wipe wipe. Mop mop mop. A germ-free life! All she was short of doin' was eatin' the soap and drinkin' the feckin' bleach! All that wasted time: dusting, making beds, polishing knobs and knockers. Ornaments in their right place. *(Pause)* The poor woman. She died from nothing. An overdose of nothing.
>
> *(He gets the Hoover; hangs the cord over a beam; makes a noose, putting it around his neck; stands up on a chair)*
>
> Billy was always her favourite. It was easy for him. *(Drinking)* I was left here to clean up the mess. *(Looks around at the state of the place)* Lately I sort of just gave up. *(He puts the plug of the hoover cord into his top pocket; he finishes the drink)* I'll miss my books. *(...)* I'll be glad when it's all over. *(Lights down)*

THE BURN VICTIM

A monologue

A woman with a Zimmer frame, she is totally covered in bandages, her face barely seen (she finds it difficult to talk).
The suggestion of a hospital corridor may be used.

Dolly enters on the right; she struggles across the stage – while speaking to the audience – and exits on the left.

DOLLY

Two of the little bastards poured the petrol. The older one threw the match. They'd seen me on the street loads of times.
'She's only a smelly wino,' said one of them, 'no one would even bother piss on her!' My teeth were rotten. My shoes were stuffed with old newspapers. My hair was filthy and I had fleas. But I didn't deserve to be set on fire. I've got 80% burns over my body.

I wasn't always an alcoholic. I went to a good school. I was very good at art and fashion. My mother always said that I'd be a famous model or a dress designer or something. She died when I was young. The lads that burnt me for fun stood and watched.

'The dirty ol' cunt is lit-up like a Christmas tree.' 'The best crack we had in ages.' 'A waste of good poxy petrol!' the third one said. They were hard men, standing there laughing. When I was 23 I got married. We had a normal, a good life. We had a little boy. Then he died.

I began to drink heavy. I'd hide the drink all around the house: in the waste bin, in the toilet cistern - I'd even take to the bed with a hot water bottle full of vodka. I'd tuck myself up and pull the covers over my head; I felt safe, like being back in the womb. I found it very hard to talk to anyone. One day I went out to get some groceries. And never went back.

I've been in here a long time. A horrible time: antiseptic bed washes, burnt skin removal. Most of my main organs are burnt away. I've hardly anything left inside me. I had to have a new rectum made. They took out the whole nine foot of colon.

Then there's my face. How would you like to run into me every morning before breakfast? I was no oil painting before; now I look like a boiled bloody lobster! Some sort of sideshow freak. Most people's nightmares end when they wake up. *(Pause)* I'm the guinea pig in here. Doctors examining me day and night; prodding and probing me.

(...) I'm not even sure what month it is. I think it's Ocvember? I get very confused. They keep filling me full of drugs. I'm blind in one eye. I have no smell. I can barely swallow. I've got a bag attached to me instead of a bowel. I have to have my food liquidized so as it doesn't block up the tube. *(...)* They said I should be dead. It's only a matter of time. *(Exits)*

THE ALCOHOLIC

A monologue

RITA is ironing. And drinking vodka. (She has clothes in a basket, folding them etc.) She drinks constantly, becoming drunker as the piece goes on. She spits on the iron to see if it's hot enough.

RITA

My bastard of a husband left me a while ago. I don't talk about it much. Let's just say, he was no good for me. We didn't see eye to eye. It took a long time for me to wake-up and smell the bloody roses.

I had my own business. A jewellery shop. I could sell sand to the Arabs, or snow to the Eskimos, if you prefer. I could sniff out a customer. Once they opened my door, I had them. *(...)* It wasn't a great area; mostly riffraff, to be honest. I looked on my shop as a little diamond in the rough.

(Pours a large drink) My doctor told me once that I have an unhealthy relationship with drink. *(Drinks)* He's dead now. Ass cancer. Who's unhealthy now! The drink takes the edge off. I'm not apologizing. It's not my fault. It's hereditary. My mother drank. Her mother drank. It's in the DNA. You could chase the gene right back to the dinosaurs. Even as a young girl I'd find myself getting over-excited with a packet of wine gums. I don't drink excessively; I drink consistently. I have hollow legs. *(...)* I stay in shape. I go to the gym. I think I look very good for my age.

Some days I used to make a big sale. That businessman looking for the perfect piece of jewellery. Bigger and dearer the better. Money no object. For his new wife; or his little secretary. *(...)* But mostly it was just earrings, chains, batteries for watches and the like. A lot of time wasters. They'd come in and just nose around. Fondling all the jewellery. Mauling the merchandise. No intention of buying anything.

They'd even try to sell me stuff. Rings, brooches, gold bracelets and the like. All left behind from the dead parents. I knew the type ... eager to get rid of the stuff; and whatever I'd offer them, they'd take. I'd give them, say, 50 quid for the lot. Later I might get 100 quid for just one bracelet! That's good business sense. Most of that sort of customer needed the money. And I was able to give it to them. I never felt guilty. I had to listen to them moan; take the risk of being able to sell the stuff on; check that it was not stolen; make sure there was no damage; that it was all genuine. A lot of stuff.

(...) Our marriage was OK in the beginning. Then I got to know him. Our sex life was the same as any other married couple: we didn't talk about it much. *(Drinks)* In the early days the sex wasn't too bad, I suppose. But in the end all he could manage was a brief erection, with medical assistance. A vagina seemed to confuse him.

I had the opportunity to meet plenty of good-looking men when I had the shop. There was one man. Indian, I think? Very handsome. Perfect smooth skin. Lovely white teeth. My husband's teeth were rotten. He never looked after them. Never once saw him flossing or using a bottle of mouth wash. Most of the time his breath smelt like a gorilla's armpit. He was never a very oral person.

(...) This Indian man would bring me in pearls to look at. Small pink pearls. Junk is all they really were. *(...)* I would give him money straight out of the till. He was always more than satisfied. I always made sure to give him my card, with my phone number, and tell him to call me at any time if he'd anything else to offer me. *(...)* I was always faithful. For as long as we were married. I never once strayed. The bloody fool that I was.

(Drinks) I have to drop in on my mam later. She's not too good on her feet anymore. 84. A bit shaky. I keep an eye on her. Cook a bit of dinner for her. I don't know what she's hanging on for. She suffered a stroke a few years ago which has rendered her totally annoying. Her will to live seems to overpower her body's desire to call it a day. Last week when I was with her, I made a classic Freudian slip. I meant to say, 'Please pass the milk,' but it came out, 'You Bitch, you ruined my childhood.'

We'll have a drink together. Actually, it's easier to understand her after she's had a few drinks. *(...)* Not to overdo it. A glass of wine. Maybe a vodka. Not to fall around the place. A pick me up; a little night cap. My husband knew nothing. Why can't a person just be left alone?

He made sure it was a messy finish. *(Pause)* Social services don't have to get involved! Treatment ... he kept at me, to get treatment, get help. *(Pause)* Oh, *I'm* the one that needs help. *(Pause)* None of it was ever *his* fault. *(Pause)* We were married, weren't we? Man and wife. That's a contract. There are certain obligations in a marriage. You can't just pack up and fuck off when you bloody well feel like it__

But he didn't give a shit about that. All he cared about was making sure I'd never see my son and grandchild again. Making sure to tell all his scummy friends what a bad a person I am.
Now my own son won't talk to me. And my little granddaughter runs the other way when she sees me. I wouldn't do anything to harm her. I love her more than life itself. *(...)* They get into everything at that age. They climb everywhere. You need eyes in the back of your head. *(Drinks)* All children have accidents.

Spreading his vicious lies. Turning everybody against me. *(...)* He wants a divorce. Shacked up with that slapper. That two-faced bitch of his. Of course, she was half my age. Perfect little tits. With a little pear shaped ass. May she give him a dose of syphilis. He'll get his comeuppance. I hope he gets cancer of the testicles, that'll be good enough for him. I hope his rotten prostrate falls out while he's having sex with the tramp. It was my shop. Mine. *My* shop! He had nothing before he married me. Nothing. The self-righteous prick. Mr. Perfect, in his perfect suit; his perfect white shirts - that I fuckin' ironed for him! His perfect hair and his perfectly polished shoes. I'm sure the fucker has OCD. *(...)*

You'd never see him have a drink too many. Or let his hair down. Oh, no - that would be too normal for him. They said I had some sort of breakdown. All I remember is running down the street in my underwear with a carving knife. Screaming. Not chasing anybody. Just running down the street with a carving knife, in my underwear, screaming.

(...) She couldn't have wanted him for his money. The tight fucker. Or his looks. The ugly bastard. If I ever see the bitch I'll tear her womb out. I'll do a homemade hysterectomy on her. Then I'll castrate him with a rusty Stanley knife. I'd like to smash his face in with this iron. But I wouldn't harm a fly. Not a fly.

My best years wasted. Flushed down the toilet. What have I got to look forward to? Surgical tights, and fuckin' Alzheimer's disease! *(Drinks)* The bastard! I gave him my best bloody years. I hope he chokes on his own vomit! What a stupid saying: 'choke on your own vomit' - what are you supposed to do, choke on somebody else's vomit!

They're all the same! They ponce around with their cheap diamonds; their imitation leather; with their false gold. And their fake tits. No class none of them. Every bit of jewellery they own on them at once. It's like throwin' pearls at swine! Out for everything they can get. Good for nothing whores, that's all they are.

Mam won't be around for much longer. Anytime soon I'd say. A house like that I could sell in a flash. I could find a nice little shop. A good area. A fresh start. *(.....)* All of them coming in to stare. Pointing the finger. Defacing my shop front.

My own son turned against me. The ungrateful shit. I ruined my body giving birth to him. The breasts sucked off me. The stretch marks. The varicose veins. You give them everything. Do everything for them. Be a mother. A nurse. A babysitter. You dress them, feed them, and wipe their arses. Put your life on hold for them. Give up on your dreams. For what. For them to grow up - and piss off!

(...) I should be in a better place. Away from the riffraff around here. *(...)* A fresh start. A classy little boutique, or maybe, a small flower shop. *(...)* I want customers with taste. A bit of breeding. *(...)* If I see the bitch I'll smack her in the teeth with a coal scuttle. Kick her in the gallbladder. Then stab her in the heart and jump up and down on her dead body. But I couldn't hurt a fly. Not a fly. Not even a little fly. *(Lights down)*

THE TOILET CLEANER

A Monologue

A room in a mental hospitall. A man dressed as a woman.

It's a funny world. Homosexuals, Heterosexuals, Bisexuals, Transsexuals. Whatever works. I'm a Transvestite. I've been cross dressing ever since I've been out of nappies. Ever since I got my first junior bra. I like to look good. Take pride in myself. Pamper myself. Most people wouldn't know fashion if came up and bit them on the bum.

I shouldn't be here. I haven't done anything wrong. It all started with the knock on the door. The TV Licence man. I whooshed him away. Fuck off - shoo, I said. The wife looked shocked and in need of a blanket. "I THOUGHT YOU BOUGHT A LICENCE!" she said. "No"- I said, "we never had a licence, except for our marriage licence, and boy that was a big mistake!" She then shouted "DUCK!" And I got hit on the head with a frozen chicken leg.

I'm not a happy man. Nor do I love my wife. Hate would be a better word. I hate her. And she hates me. At least it's mutual. She stopped talking to me a long time ago. Ever since she caught me bringing home a packet of tampons. She's let herself go. Hardly spends any time on her hair or her makeup. But she won't take advice from me. She knows everything. She's the boss. She wears the trousers.

Most of the time she spends in the kitchen. She can't cook for shite. She cremates everything. She shouldn't be allowed anywhere near food. She's lethal. She can deflavourise anything. She gave me a bleedin' ulcer with all the crap she cooks. My stomach was swollen. It was like I was pregnant. I had to have it taken out. I still have the scar across my belly. My insides are ruined because of her. My tummy in turmoil; my belly in rebellion. Every time I fart, my bumhole feels like it's on fire.

If you haven't got your health nothing else matters. You never appreciate what you have 'till it's gone. The wife calls me a hypochondriac. I'm not a hypochondriac. It's just that she made me feel sick all the time. Thank god for medical science. Just look what they can do nowadays: Botox; breast implants; hormone replacement. You know there are people walking around with hardly anything they started out with.

I'm a writer, well, actually I'm a toilet cleaner, but I write a lot in my spare time. I've just finished translating the works of James Joyce into English. I'm a very creative person. I use the left side of my brain a lot. The wife doesn't understand. She only uses the right side of her brain.

I prefer to be in here than at home. It's better than cleaning toilets. And listening to the wife nag. We never have any fun. We never laugh. Except when she broke her foot when one of her homemade meringues fell on it. I laughed then aright. Until she hit me again. I should have left her years ago. Sex was never any good. She's like a bloody nun. She never tries anything new. She blames me, says I suffer from impotence. I do not! I suffer from her incompetence.

(...) I was excited about my big day in court. I spent hours in the bathroom getting ready. I waxed my legs. Plucked my eyebrows. Shaved my armpits. And put on the wife's new red dress; topped off with a pair of black tights and one of her fancy braziers stuffed with cotton balls. And away I went. A waste of time. The judge hardly noticed me. He went on about '__if you have a television set, you must also have a television licence__' He bored the hole off me. Before I knew it - I fixed my cleavage, leaped up, and took a run at him with my hatpin, stabbing him in the eyeball! He let out a almighty yelp, jumping up nearly blowing his little wig off! I was sent in here to get help.

When they let me out I'm going have the full operation. Nigel, my cellmate - they don't like me calling it a cell - Nigel, my roommate, say's when we get out, I can come and move in with him. He's a lovely young man. A transsexual. He said he'd show me how it's done. With a razor blade and some Detol. And he has a 52 inch TV. With all the digital channels. I said I'd give it a go.

THE DENTIST

W. C. Dangleberry, is the Dentist. He is old, with glasses; he moves funny, has a way about him. (Talks only to Larry)

Larry, is the Patient. A lively young man; impressionable. (Talks to Dentist, and to Audience)

Larry is seated in the chair. The Dentist is bent over him with his back to the audience.

Dentist

(Moving away) Haven't seen your grandfather in a while. How is his set of false teeth?

Larry

(Fixing the sheet over himself in the chair) Not great! He's been dead now over twenty years!

Dentist

Still, those teeth were top-notch craftsmanship. I bet they're still in great shape. Were they buried with him by any chance? A lot of people bring them back in to me, you know? I'm able to recondition them.

Larry

Jeez, if I knew that I would have kept them. *(Talks to the audience)* What a man. He tells me loads of interesting things like that. (*The dentist moves over to his work place*) He's over seventy. His name is Dangleberry. He talks to himself, forgets things, and even has bad breath ... but I could never leave him. I've been going to him since I was a kid. I love him. He's the BEST. I let no one else near my gums.

Dentist

(Not sure if Larry said something to him) What was that?

Larry

No, nothing!

Dentist

(Coming back with the drill) Yeah, the families sell the teeth back to me; I clean them up, make them fit someone else's mouth. It's easy. Open-up now. *(He looks inside Larry's mouth)* Peoples jawbones are nearly the same size. A little filing, that's all that's needed. I think a good set of false teeth not put to good use is a crying shame. The workmanship alone; the time and skill involved. People take that for granted.

Larry

(He talks to the audience) What a clever man. This is what I'm talking about. You don't get this kind of expertise everyday. *(Pause)* His son's also a dentist. He works here as well. *(Noise of the drill)* But I only go to him; the father; the original. He taught Junior everything he knows. *(Larry's told to rinse)* The son's always busy ... his waiting room's always packed. People have to ring for an appointment weeks in advance. *(The dentist continues drilling in between Larry talking)* Now with this guy, there's never any waiting. That's good business. Don't have customers waiting.

Dentist

(Giving him some cotton wool) Now suck on this bit of candyfloss. *(He moves away, working on something)*

Larry

(Continuing talking to audience) And he spends over forty-five minutes each time with me. The new ones would never do that. They like the money. In and out. Next patient. The money's all they care about. *(He takes out the wool)* In the last four months I've had six teeth removed. Only one of them was bad. But I let him take them out. It was better to take them out. Complications could set in at any time.

Dentist

(Suddenly) I remember your grandfather! Bald, wasn't he. Wore glasses like binoculars; a head like a snooker ball, except for the hair growin' outa his nose. That's bad news about him, all right. He was a good patient. Never a peep out of him. He had a mouth full of molars in his day. Mighty they were. It must've took me over five hours to get the suckers out! *(Pause)* Teeth are funny like that. Pearly white on top, but underneath they're rotten to the core. One day they're fine, next thing - all you can feel is the pain.

Larry

(Still to audience) Now, any other dentist, even his son, would have left me with those bad teeth. And then one day they'd start to bleed ... to hurt me ... begin to smell ... to rot in my head ... and then they'd all fall out. He saved me from that. He was on the ball.

Dentist

It's not real lead they use in fillings anymore. It's only plaster. But I still use lead. It's the best. It lasts forever. Them teeth you've left ... they're super strong. You could chew toffee bars all day long - hell, you could chew through iron bars, if you had to! *(Rambling)* Like in the coffin's they made in the old days; they would last forever, no chance of the maggots gettin' in near you. Not like them new ones, only bloomin' plywood.

Larry

(To Dentist) Dr. Dangleberry ... you're a wise man. Lead does last a long time. Sure don't they put it on roofs and things? People even try and rob it.

Dentist

You be smart, kid - keep your mouth closed when you're around people you don't know. *(...)* Ever been married Larry?

Larry

Eh - No Doc, not yet!

Dentist

Keep it that way. You're one of the lucky ones. If only I'd known myself. Married life isn't all it's cracked up to be. *(Pause)* Some nights you just don't want to go home. *(Pause)* They nag, you know - a lot - and that's only starters. She'll be there at home keepin' watch for me; waitin' to pounce. I have to say it, but I feel more at home with my drill and my chair.

Larry

But Doc - you're wife's dead - the last four years!

Dentist

Are you sure about that? *(...)* They all want me to retire. Give it all up. I think my son wants the business to himself.

Larry

(To audience) Bloody no-good-opportunist that Dangleberry Jr. No respect for old age ... or the wisdom that goes with it. *(...)* He *can't* retire. I've been going to him since I was a kid. We get on well together. He knows the drill. And if I don't want gas ... or an injection ... that's ok too. And he's not afraid to make a mistake, take out a wrong tooth. I like that. It shows he's human. Not just another stranger in a white coat looking down your throat.

Dentist

I don't want to retire ... that's the end of everything ... you're left with too much time on your hands ... And before you know it they'll be sending you to the funny farm. *(Pause)* Teeth is all I know. *(Confiding in Larry)* It all started with this old girl I had in the chair a few months back. She was a good-looker in her day. Seen it all. Two wars. A couple of husbands. Now she'd only two front teeth left in her head, like a rat. And wore perfume that smelt like fly killer. *(Pause)* So I gave her the gas ... and then what do you think she did? ... She only started to take her clothes off! First the blouse ... then her bra. I didn't know what to do ... So I gave her more gas - and the old dear slept like a baby, dribbling and everything. And then, goddamn it, if she didn't go and die on me!

Larry

Jesus!

Dentist

Now they won't let me do any of the real stuff anymore. After all them years. No more gas. No more needles. Not even one extraction. This is the last time you'll be seeing me kid. They'll only let me work on the sets of false teeth now. My son will handle all the other stuff.

Larry

(To Dentist) Bloody hell! No respect. *(Pause)* All them years of hard work you put in here ... and now they want to get rid of you ... just *one* little mistake! It's not right. *(Very agitated)* And what about me? What will I do? Who'll look after me! *(An idea hits home)* Would you be able to make me a set of your false teeth?

Dentist

Sure, kid. That's no problem. I'd be proud to. *(Gets rid of Larry) (Shouts after him)* But somebody else is gonna have to remove them teeth you have left!

(Lights down)

(Sometime later. The Dentist is fixing false teeth. Drinking mouthwash; trying out the false teeth; coughing, spitting etc. Larry enters; he looks a bit different.)

Larry

(Talking funny) What's up doc! *(Pause)* I see your sons waiting room is still chock-a-block.

Dentist

(Confused) Ah ... Larry, my young man - take a seat.

Larry

(Eager) I'm ready for you Doc. *(Sits in the chair and puts the sheet over himself)* All the teeth are gone. Easy it was ... with a Stanley knife. And a pliers. I just had to wait to let the blood clot; and my gums harden. Have a look at my handy work.

Dentist

(Shocked) Well, kid - lets have a see. *(Has a good look in his mouth)* Hell ... you've done a good job. A damn good job. My son wouldn't have been able to do any better. Even with all his fancy hi-tech equipment. A Stanley knife, you say?

Larry

And a pliers!

Dentist

The old ways are always best. *(...)* I thought him everything he knows ... and that's the thanks I get ... *(Rambling)* one little mistake ... what did the old dear have to take her clothes off for? ... Yep, no doubt about it, you've done a great job. *(Fumbles for a set of false teeth)* And now look what I have for you! *(Pause)* I can also give you ten quid for any of the old lead you have left.

Larry

Here you go doc. *(Takes out a bag with teeth in it)* They're all yours! *(Excited)* Oh, my God! You made these for me! They're really mine? *(Examining the set of teeth)* They're PERFECT! Top-notch craftsmanship. I LOVE them!

Dentist

I'm glad, kid. That's all I need to hear. I had pleasure making them for you. You have always been a nice young man. Respectful. *(Moving Larry nearer the door)* Real good work. Go on home now, and tell your grandfather I was asking for him. *(Larry exits)* You have talent, kid. *(Shouts after him)* Did you never think of becoming a dentist yourself?

Larry

(Larry comes back) Oh, No! I was always just happy being a patient! *(...)* I love them. I really love them. I'm gonna go around smiling all the time. Everywhere. I don't care if people think I'm an idiot. *(Still excited. He won't leave)* And at night I will put them in a glass of bleach. Oh, yes!, I'm gonna take real good care of my new teeth. *(Giving the old man a hug)* Thank you. Thank you. *(Pause)* Some days I won't even wear them at all. *(Larry exits)*

Dentist

(Flustered. He sits in his chair. Has a drink. Keeping his eye on the door.) Dead four years! ... Who's dead four years?
(Lights down)

Printed in Great Britain
by Amazon

47809690R00057